This Book Belongs To

Lauren Wanlass

The Wind in the Willows

THE OPEN ROAD

Based on the original story by Kenneth Grahame

Retold by Andrea Stacy Leach
Illustrated by Holly Hannon

McClanahan Book Company, Inc.
New York

"Ratty," said the Mole, one bright summer morning, "I want to ask you a favor. Will you take me to visit Mr. Toad? I've heard so much about him."

"Why certainly," said the Water Rat, jumping to his feet. "Get the boat out, and we'll paddle up there at once. It's never a wrong time to call on Toad. Always good-tempered, always glad to see you, always sorry when you go!"

"He must be a very nice animal," said Mole as he got into the boat.

"He is the best of animals," replied Rat. "Perhaps he's not very clever—but we can't all be geniuses."

Rounding a bend in the river, they came to a handsome old house of red brick. "There's Toad Hall," said the Rat.

When they came to Toad's boathouse they went ashore and strolled across the lawn in search of Toad.

They found him resting in a wicker garden chair with a large map spread out on his knees.

"Hooray!" Toad cried, jumping up. "This is splendid! I was just going to send a boat down the river for you, Ratty, to bring you here at once. I want you badly—both of you. I have something to show you. Come with me and you shall see!"

Toad led the way to a large yard. There they saw a gypsy cart, looking brand new, painted a canary yellow with red wheels.

"There you are!" cried the Toad. "There's real life for you. The open road, the dusty highway, camps, villages! Travel, change, excitement! The whole world before you. We start this afternoon."

Rat began to protest, but Mole was quite excited by the idea of traveling. Toad reassured Rat that the cart would be very comfortable. "You see, everything you can possibly want," said Toad. "Little sleeping bunks, a little table, a cooking stove and lots of pots and pans!" When they were quite ready, Toad led his companions to the field to get the old gray horse. It took a great deal of work to catch the horse, but at last it was caught and harnessed, and they set off, all talking at once.

It was a golden afternoon. Birds whistled. Travelers waved and said, "Good-day." Late in the evening, they pulled off the road, tired and happy.

After supper, Toad said sleepily, "Well, good night, you fellows. This is the real life for a gentleman!"

Toad slept very soundly. No amount of shaking could rouse him the next morning. So Rat fed the horse and got things ready for

breakfast. Mole trudged off to the nearest
village to buy the things Toad had forgotten to
provide.

"What a pleasant, easy life this is!" said Toad
when he woke up.

The next evening they camped again in a
field. This time the two guests made sure that
Toad did his share of the work. And when the
time came to start the next morning, Toad was
no longer so keen on the outdoor life.

When they finally came to the main road, they began to hear a faint hum behind them. Glancing back, they saw a small cloud of dust approaching.

Then, suddenly, a blast of wind and a whirl of sound made them jump for the nearest ditch.

"Beep, beep!" sounded harshly in their ears, while a cloud of dust covered them. For a moment, they had a glimpse of a magnificent car. Then it disappeared into the distance.

The old gray horse, very upset, reared and plunged. Despite all Mole's efforts to calm him, he drove the cart backwards toward the deep ditch at the side of the road. Crash!

The canary-colored cart lay in the ditch.
The Rat jumped up and down in the road.
"You villains!" he shouted. He shook both his
fists. "You scoundrels, you—you—road hogs!"

But Toad sat in the middle of the dusty road. "Glorious sight!" he murmured dreamily. "The only way to travel. O bliss! O beep, beep! O my! To think I never knew! All these wasted years. But now, what dust clouds shall spring up behind me as I speed on my reckless way!"

"What shall we do with him?" asked Mole.

"Nothing at all," replied Rat. "He has now got a new craze."

An inspection of the cart showed them that it could travel no longer. The Rat took the horse by the head. "Come on," he said grimly. "It's five or six miles to the nearest town, and we shall just have to walk."

"Now, look here, Toad!" said the Rat sharply. "As soon as we get to town, you'll have to go to the police and complain about that car. Then you'll have to arrange for the cart to be fixed."

Toad murmured, still dreamy eyed, "Me *complain* about that beautiful vision! Fix the cart! I'm done with carts."

Rat turned from him in despair. "You see what it is," he said to Mole. "He's quite hopeless. I give up."

When they reached the town they left the horse at a stable and took a train that dropped them near Toad Hall.

Rat and Mole escorted the spellbound Toad to his door and pushed him inside. Then they got into their boat and rowed home. At a very late hour, they sat down to supper in their own cozy riverside kitchen. Rat was happy at last.

The following evening, the Mole was sitting on the riverbank fishing. The Rat came along to find him.

"Heard the news?" Rat asked. "Toad went up to town on an early train this morning. And he has ordered a large and very expensive motor-car!"